Bonnie,
Our Backyard Bunny

Written by
Susan Letendre

Illustrated by
Saulo Serrano

Saulo Serrano Serrano
31-julio-1948-Cuba

To Olivia, my city bunny,

who inspires my every good word and deed.

I'm going to tell you a story. This is a true story about a rabbit who lives behind our house. Her name is Bonnie, Bonnie Our Backyard Bunny.

I first met Bonnie a year ago. She was hopping around in a rain shower.

Now, most bunnies don't like rain much. Bonnie loves rain. She loves how rain makes everything greener. Everything that is good for Bonnie to eat is green, so Bonnie's favorite color is green. In her heart, because bunnies don't talk out loud, she says,

"Thank you, rain!"

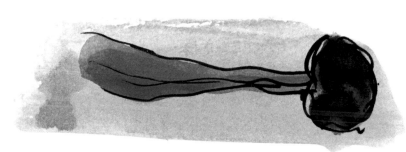

Do you know what happens when an animal eats, and her belly takes all that it needs from the food? We are animals, too, and we do this. We usually go into a small room in the house, shut the door, and sit on a special chair to do it. But other animals do it outside. Do you know what it is?

Right, poop. And the poop that some animals make, like bunny poop, is the very best thing for plants. So, as Bonnie hops around the yard, eating and pooping, saying "thank you" to rain, she is feeding the plants with her poop. Then the plants grow faster and bigger, and Bonnie gets more to eat.

"Thank you, poop!"

As Bonnie hopped around in the rain, she wiggled her nose at a big fat worm. When it rains, and the ground gets full of water, worms come out so they can breathe… just like Bonnie breathes, and you breathe, and me, too!

Worms are wonderful. They make tunnels in the ground by eating dirt. Then they poop out the back end. And this worm poop is wonderful food for plants! Some farmers even grow worms just so they can get their poop! They call it "black gold". Then some farmers sell this "black gold" in little bags, so people can take it home and put it on their plants.

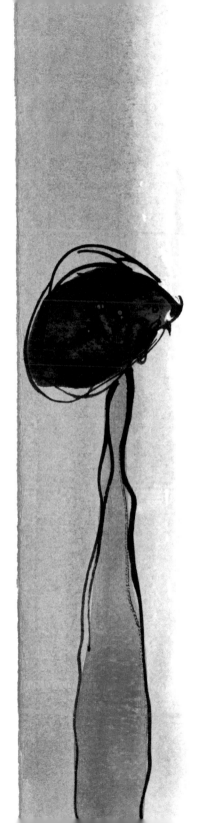

Do you have a worm bin at home? Worm bins are big boxes that are worm houses. Worms live in there, and people feed them food they don't eat, like carrot tops, and orange peels, and banana peels. And the worms will turn it into "black gold" right in the box.

Thank you, worms!

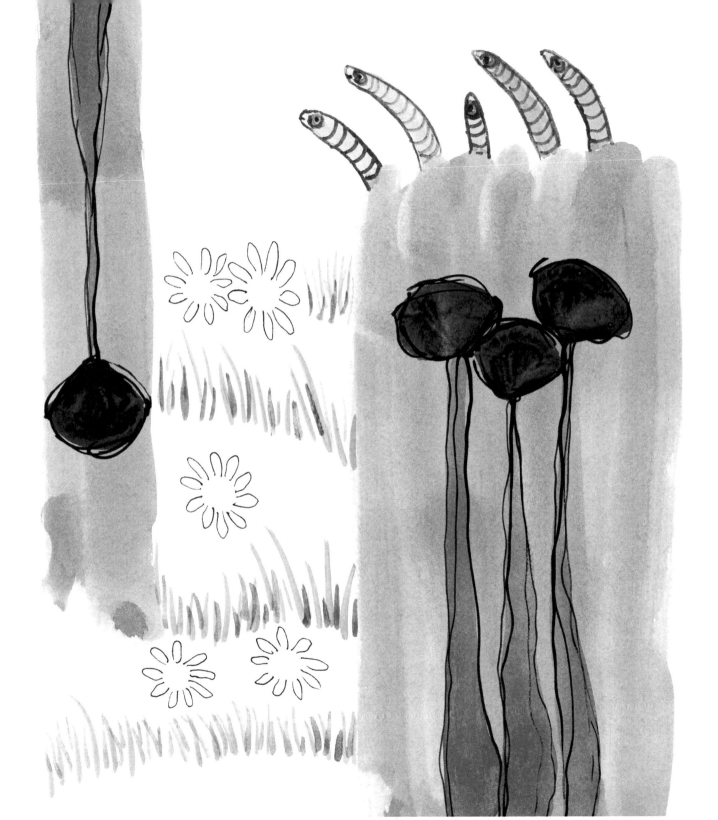

On this day, Bonnie was eating her favorite food, clover. Clover feeds the ground, so that the ground can make food for other plants. As Bonnie ate the clover flowers, she spread seeds around the yard so that more clover could grow.

Thank you, clover!
Thank you, Bonnie!

Bonnie's second favorite food is wild morning glory vines. Morning glory vines climb up other flowers and sometimes make them sick.

So, as Bonnie sits among the flowers, she munches happily on the wild morning glory vines. And the other flowers are happy, too.

Thank you, Bonnie!

And thank you, morning glory vines, for feeding our bunny!

Now, Bonnie is a very healthy bunny, because she is outside all day, hopping around, and eating all the things that are good for bunnies.

But sometimes, just like you and me, she gets a tummyache.

When she does, she likes to chew on chamomile flowers. Chamomile flowers are good for us, too, when we have a tummyache. When Bonnie feels better, she says,

"Thank you chamomile flowers!"

As Bonnie chewed on some chamomile, she heard a loud buzz and picked her head up just in time. A big, fat bee was about to bounce into her big bunny ear. The bee was covered with yellow flower pollen and she could barely bumble.

This bee had visited lots of flowers that day, getting nectar to make honey. Each flower stuck yellow pollen to her legs. When the bee visited the next flower, she left some of that pollen on the new flower.

Flowers use this pollen to make fruits and vegetables. Then the fruits and vegetables make seeds. Do you know what seeds grow into? That's right. More plants, more flowers. This bee was doing a great job!

Thank you bee!

This is how it works:

The more seeds, the more flowers…

the more flowers the more nectar…

the more nectar, the more bees…

the more bees, the more honey…

the more honey, the more bees…

the more bees, the more seeds.

Everything circles round and round.

Because EVERYTHING in Bonnie's

world fits together.

Just like in OUR world.

Some very tiny animals drink from flowers, too. Bonnie's favorite tiny animals are hummingbirds. She loves to watch them sparkle in the air like flying jewels.

Hummingbirds build nests in our yard because everything they need grows there. They make their nests from leaves, bark, and moss. And then they put dandelion fluff down inside to make the nest soft for their babies.

Thank you, dandelions!

Then the mother hummingbird
sticks it all together with…
do you know what?

Spider webs!

Thank you, spiders!

Now Bonnie's day is ending. Suddenly there is a loud noise of chirping and squawking in the trees. Bonnie dives for cover just as a big hawk swoops down from the sky. Phew!!! Hawks like to eat bunnies. But the birds warned her!

Thank you, birds!

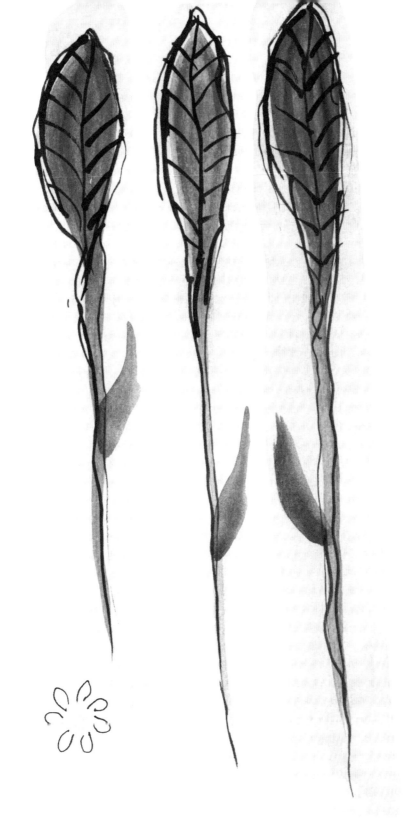

But wait a minute! Hawks make sure that just the right number of animals live in our backyard so that everyone has plenty of room and plenty to eat.

Thank you, hawk!

Bonnie is now pretty tired from her busy day, and it's time for her to go to bed. She hops down into her warm burrow, just behind her cousin, Betty Bunny, and just in front of her brother, Benny Bunny.

And as they all snuggle close for the night,
Bonnie closes her eyes and thinks about
all the wonderful things in her world.
And, in her heart, she says,

Thank you!

A community birthed this book.

First, there was Claire Sartori, who opened the portal through which this book flowed. Then my beloved Cuban friends, who have hearts as wide as the world: Saulo Serrano, of course, and Edelso Moret, Carmen Pérez, Polo Cabrer Topez, Rev. Suarez. To Witness for Peace New England, that made it possible for me to travel to the enchanted island. To the people who raised me up in peace and justice: my mother, John & Mary B Hall, Art Stein, Paul Magno, and a host of others. To more of my family: Peter Letendre & Linda Howell; my son and daughter-in-law, René & Krisi Letendre; Karen Williams & Bob Schwartz, Clark Letendre. And to wonderful friends who held my hand, or shook me by the shoulders, and told me I could do this: SE Fox, Ginny Ricciardi, Pat Schneider, Bonnie Phinney. And to my magical writer's group: Nicole Spaulding, Kate Vivian, Shirley Eastham, and Jean Zipke. And to Annapoorne Coangelo, who sent me love and cheer through the ether. And to John Lee, who not only sent great financial support, but also a piece of a Douglas fir tree, to remind me that I, like the fir, am held up by a collective. (The moss on the tree is still alive after months in a winter-dry house, even though I mistakenly sprayed it with the Listerine I spray on my gardening pants to keep the tics off.)

To Jill Shorrock, graphic artist, whose extraordinary skills put the words and pictures on the pages, and then jiggled them until they breathed and hopped.

To my longest-lasting friend and encouraging editor, Anne Marshall and my fellow Cuba traveler, Meredith Reiniger, whose reviews were oh-so kind and helpful.

And to the 90 people who became part of this book by giving financial support and encouraging words.

And to the real backyard bunny, who trusted me enough to let me observe her for three years and become part of her world.

All these folk have taught me so much about community, and about creating a caring society. These lessons have informed this small tale that Bonnie tells.

THANK YOU!

About the Author...

Susan Letendre is an environmental educator, a storyteller, and a peace and justice activist. She believes in the connectedness of all things. She lives in a tiny house, on a tiny lake, in the tiniest state of Rhode Island.

About the Artist...

Saulo Serrano is one of Cuba's best-loved, and well-known, artists and educators. All his work illustrates that everything has a place, and everything fits together. He lives and works among trees and flowers in Havana, Cuba.

CPSIA information can be obtained
at www.ICGtesting.com
Printed in the USA
LVXC02n0310051215
465138LV00021B/122

* 9 7 8 0 9 9 6 2 1 5 2 0 6 *